# Stories from My Father

# Publication Information



First Edition 2024

Cover design by Geoffrey K. Maiyoh

Published by Geoffrey K. Maiyoh

ISBN: 9798230563594

"A journey through the landscapes of life, woven with values, family, and legacy."

# From a Father's Heart

As fathers, we tell stories not just to entertain, but to pass on wisdom—guiding the next generation to find strength and inspiration in life's journey."

— Dr. G. Maiyoh

# CONTENTS

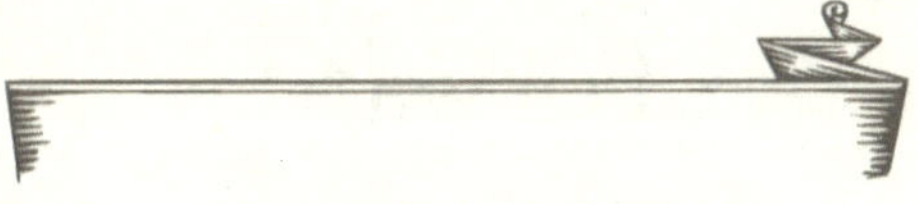

# Dedication

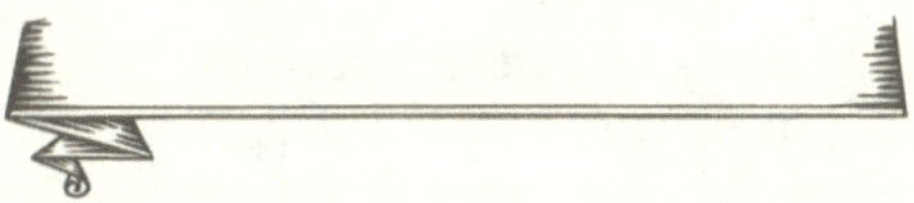

*This book is lovingly dedicated to my amazing wife, Jenniffer, and our wonderful children, Ethan, Ryan, and Kinsley—thank you for being my companions on this incredible journey through life.*

# Forward

Our dad loves to tell stories. Whether it's a tale about a magical river or a young inventor in Nairobi, his stories are always filled with adventure and lessons that stay with us. But one of the stories in this book is extra special because we were part of it!

Yes, the Johannesburg adventure is based on a trip we took as a family. It's about the time we explored new places, braved the rain, met a gorilla at the zoo, and discovered so much about each other along the way. That story isn't just from his imagination—it's our true adventure brought to life on these pages.

This book combines all the wonder, inspiration, and fun we feel when Dad shares his stories with us. We hope you'll enjoy these journeys as much as we do and maybe even find a bit of your own family's story in them.

With love,
Ethan, Ryan, and Kinsley

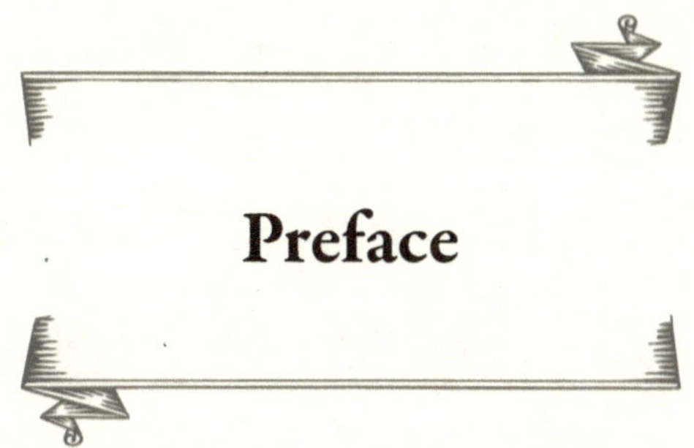

# Preface

These seven stories are a reflection of my love for storytelling and the deep connection I feel to the landscapes, traditions, and evolving future of Kenya. Each tale is a journey—some magical, some grounded in reality, but all woven with the common threads of resilience, discovery, and community. From the mystical powers of Kabosie, guardian of the Yala River, to the tech-savvy brilliance of Oliver in Nairobi, these characters represent the heart of a people who face challenges with courage and embrace the unknown with hope.

In crafting these stories, I wanted to highlight the rich diversity of our experiences, from the legends that shape our past to the innovations that point toward our future. The journeys in these pages are meant not only to entertain but also to offer insights, spark curiosity, and foster a sense of pride in the unique blend of culture and progress that defines Africa today.

I invite you to immerse yourself in these worlds and discover, as I did while writing them, the beauty of stories that connect us all. Thank you for joining me on this adventure.

Warm regards,

Dr. Geoffrey K. Maiyoh

# Introduction

Welcome to a collection of stories that celebrate the spirit of adventure, tradition, and innovation, all set against the rich and diverse backdrop of Africa and beyond. In these pages, you'll journey from the iconic Maasai Mara, where a brave young princess embarks on a thrilling safari (*Safari Adventure with the Lionhearted Princess of Nandiland*), to the vibrant streets of Kisumu, where an ancient necklace carries a legacy of courage (*The Necklace of Courage*).

From the majestic landscapes of Kenya, the stories expand to international horizons. Travel to Johannesburg in *A Johannesburg Adventure*, where a family discovers the wonders of the city and its cultural treasures. In *A Tech Whiz in Nairobi: The Future is Here*, you'll follow a young prodigy whose groundbreaking innovations take him from the heart of Nairobi's tech scene to the renowned academic institutions of Boston.

Each story not only offers a unique adventure but also weaves in themes of courage, family, and the blend of tradition with modernity. You will meet characters who challenge the world around them—whether it's through mystical connections to nature, athletic prowess, or technological genius. These tales highlight the importance of heritage while also embracing the future, offering readers a chance to reflect on their own journeys.

As you turn the pages, I invite you to immerse yourself in the wonders of these settings and the hearts of the people who live within them. May you find inspiration in these stories and enjoy the adventure as much as I did while crafting them.

# A Tech Whiz in Nairobi: The Future is here

Oliver grew up in the heartlands of Uasin Gishu, attending one of the region's most prestigious public schools. His parents chose the name "Oliver" with intention, as it symbolized wisdom and insight—qualities they wished for their son. From a young age, Oliver lived up to the name. Gifted with a sharp intellect, he excelled effortlessly in every subject. He also had a singular dream: to become a doctor. Childhood memories of visiting clinics with his mother and watching doctors work left a deep impression on him. Their skill and compassion inspired him, and the noble idea of healing others became his guiding ambition. But life, as it often does, had other plans.

During his high school years, Oliver's natural curiosity grew beyond medicine. His mind, sharp and adaptable, soaked up knowledge like a sponge. Mathematics, biology, physics, and even art and design fascinated him. His teachers marveled at his versatility—he wasn't just good; he was exceptional in everything he touched. Yet, while others praised his potential, Oliver felt the pressure mounting. His once-clear path to becoming a doctor started to blur.

One day, during a family dinner, Oliver's father, a self-taught engineer with a love for machines, casually dropped an idea that would forever alter Oliver's course.

"Son, have you ever thought about robotics? AI?" his father asked, as though it were the most natural question in the world. "You've always been good with your hands, building things. Medical robots—they're going to change everything."

The thought struck Oliver like a jolt of electricity. Robotics? Artificial intelligence? These were fields he knew little about. But from that moment on, they dominated his thoughts. He was suddenly at a crossroads, no longer sure which path to follow. Medicine was his dream, but what about the future his father spoke of? A world where machines could help doctors diagnose and treat diseases faster, better?

The uncertainty gnawed at him, but he pushed through, excelling in school despite his confusion. His friends and teachers often told him how lucky he was to be good at everything. But to Oliver, his success only deepened the dilemma. Should he become a doctor? An engineer? Perhaps a designer—after all, his art teacher insisted he had the talent to make it big in design.

When he completed high school, Oliver received a letter of acceptance from University of the next Generation (UnGen), an international university renowned for nurturing the world's brightest minds. It offered a unique seven-year program—an intensive course that combined medicine, robotics, and computer engineering. The catch? The specialization would be decided in the final year. For the first three years, students would cover foundational sciences, before diving into robotics, medicine, and AI. The last two years were where it got exciting: students would work on projects that tailored their final course path based on individual strengths and interests. Until recently, UnGen was merely a concept in the mind of a prominent Silicon Valley tech billionaire with significant global influence. At the recently concluded World Conference on Robotics and Artificial Intelligence, he successfully persuaded world leaders to collaborate on launching UnGen—an international, borderless institution. UnGen draws expertise and students from across the globe, with the primary mission of training the next generation of professionals across all major disciplines to harness the power of robotics and AI to enhance and accelerate the quality of services worldwide.

Oliver's mind raced. It was the perfect opportunity, yet seven years felt like an eternity in the span of a human life. Seven years of pressure, competition, and discovery.

"Take the leap," his father urged. "You've got the talent. Find out where it can take you."

His mother, ever the voice of reason, gently reminded him, "You can still follow the path to healing, even with machines by your side."

And so, with equal parts excitement and trepidation, Oliver accepted the challenge.

The first three years at UnGen flew by in a whirlwind of lectures, labs, and late-night study sessions. Oliver found himself among some of the brightest minds from all over the world. He excelled in the dreaded Anatomy, Biochemistry and Physiology just as he had always imagined. But as he dove deeper into robotics and computer engineering, a new fascination began to take root.

By his fourth year, when robotics and medicine merged in the curriculum, Oliver found himself engrossed in concepts and projects that combined artificial intelligence with medicine. His project ideas were bold—machines that could not only assist doctors but potentially surpass current human capabilities in diagnosing complex diseases. His designs weren't just innovative; they were groundbreaking.

The fifth year introduced artificial intelligence in a way that made his previous work feel like child's play.

As he undertook his clinical rotations in the fifth and sixth years, Oliver became a deeply troubled man. His biggest source of unease was not the grueling nature of the course or the challenging materials. Nor was it the difficulty in relating to the consultant doctors who, often due to the immense pressure of their work, could be less than patient. He had quickly adapted to the high-stakes environment, where both patients and their families harbored intense expectations. Oliver had learned to maintain a calm, objective demeanor even in the most stressful situations. On two occasions, he had been scolded in front of patients and their relatives, yet he did not let this shatter his resolve. Overall, his seniors regarded him as an exceptional clinician with sound skills.

However, despite the professional growth, Oliver was haunted by a deep sense of inadequacy every time he returned to his empty apartment. The primary source of his despair was not the rigors of his training but the harsh reality of cancer. Time and again, he had watched patients—who had come to the hospital filled with hope after receiving their diagnoses—waste away, their conditions deteriorating rapidly. The majority of these patients presented with advanced-stage disease—often stage III or IV—when treatment options were limited, and the prognosis grim. These late-stage diagnoses left him deeply troubled, as he understood that the delays in diagnosis often made effective treatment impossible.

He had noticed a troubling trend—certain types of cancer were more prevalent and deadlier, often diagnosed at advanced stages when treatment options were limited. From the highly experienced oncologist, Dr. Shah, Oliver learned that some cancers were notoriously difficult to diagnose early. Dr. Shah had explained that pancreatic cancer was the most elusive, often referred to as a "silent killer." Early-stage pancreatic tumors don't typically show up on imaging tests, and by the time symptoms appear, the disease is usually advanced. Dr. Shah further elaborated that renal (kidney) cancer, ovarian cancer, liver cancer, and lung cancer followed close behind in terms of diagnostic difficulty, each presenting unique challenges that delayed early detection.

Oliver had also gained significant insight while working with people living with HIV and AIDS (PLWHA). He was saddened to learn that despite the advances in antiretroviral therapy (ART) prolonging their lives, the immunosuppressed state in these patients increased their risk of developing various cancers. The HIV virus itself, particularly with the human papillomavirus (HPV) or Kaposi's sarcoma-associated herpesvirus (KSHV) co-infections, could trigger the development of malignancies. He learnt that common cancers among PLWHA included Kaposi's sarcoma, non-Hodgkin lymphoma, and cervical cancer, further complicating their treatment.

The biggest heartache for Oliver, however, remained the staggering number of late diagnoses. He knew all too well that when cancer is detected at a late stage, treatment options narrow drastically, and survival rates plummet. Poor prognosis became an unfortunate reality for many of his patients.

Yet, Dr. Shah's teachings offered a glimmer of hope. He emphasized the importance of early intervention, particularly through surgery. "If we catch these tumors early, before they metastasize, and surgically remove them completely, then we've essentially cured the patient," Dr. Shah had said. The challenge, of course, was detecting the cancer in its early, more treatable stages. Dr. Shah stressed the significance of complete surgical excision of cancerous tissue, noting that any residual malignant cells could lead to relapse and further spread.

Over the course of his clinical years, Oliver had witnessed many patient fatalities. But one case weighed especially heavy on his heart—the loss of his close friend Jared, with whom he had once played high school soccer. Jared had been more than a teammate; he had been Oliver's captain and one of the brightest, most charismatic people he had known. Jared, despite excelling academically, had chosen to pursue business after high school – a decision well backed by his excellence not only in business education during early years but also in Commerce as a specialty later in his 3$^{rd}$ and 4$^{th}$ years of high school. His ventures saw him quickly establishing four thriving companies that specialized in product distribution. Oliver remained close to him, not just because of their deep friendship but because Jared's businesses provided Oliver with an easy and cost-effective way to acquire materials for his numerous medical robotics trial projects.

Yet Jared's success came at a cost. He had developed a dangerous lifestyle, becoming a heavy drinker and smoker. Oliver's friend had started with regular cigarettes, then graduated to cigars, and eventually moved on to vaping. Despite Oliver's repeated attempts to warn him about the dangers of these habits, Jared remained indifferent. He would brush off the concern with a laugh, comparing Oliver's pleas to the exaggerated warnings of an overzealous insurance salesman. But, as fate would have it, life can be unforgiving. On Oliver's most recent visit to Jared's luxurious home, something unsettling caught his attention—Jared was wheezing. Though he wanted to remain a polite guest, Oliver couldn't shake the uneasy feeling. However, as he prepared to leave, Jared confided in him about his increasing fatigue and shortness of breath. He had also become noticeably thinner, though Oliver wasn't too surprised, knowing Jared's erratic workout routines. Jared had always pushed himself to extremes—two years earlier, he had taken up bodybuilding as a marketing strategy for his companies and, before that, marathon running to prove his endurance.

Concerned, Oliver asked Jared to share more about his health and fitness. That's when he learned his friend had quit bodybuilding due to worsening chest pains, fatigue, and persistent shortness of breath. Jared, ever the optimist, downplayed his symptoms, but Oliver knew better. He urged Jared to come to the hospital for tests the next morning. Jared, however, had a flight to Beijing for a business trip that would keep him away for at least two weeks.

"I promise I'll see you as soon as I get back," Jared had said, his voice laced with the breathlessness that Oliver could no longer ignore.

Weeks passed, and Jared's condition deteriorated rapidly. Upon his return from China, he finally agreed to undergo tests. Already fearing the worst, Oliver scheduled a series of tests for Jared, including a low-dose CT scan to check for lung cancer and a biopsy for further investigation. The results confirmed Oliver's fears: Not only did Jared have lung cancer but it was already at stage IV, with metastases to his liver and bones. What caught Oliver off guard was Jared's response when asked how long he had been smoking. It was unbelievable—Jared had picked up the habit just before high school. One of his parents' neighbors had casually offered him a puff of a cigarette, and from that moment, the neighbor became unusually friendly, pretending to mentor Jared in things like driving and mechanics. All of this happened right under his parents' radar. Jared thought he was getting a great deal, but in hindsight, he should have thought twice. Now, years of smoking had taken a devastating toll on his health.

By the time the diagnosis was confirmed, it was too late for curative treatment. The cancer was advanced and inoperable. Desperate for a chance at survival, Jared's family arranged for him to be flown to India, where he could receive cutting-edge care. Oliver coordinated with oncologists abroad, hoping for a miracle. Jared underwent aggressive treatments, including chemotherapy and targeted therapy, but his body was too frail to withstand the onslaught.

Less than two months after his diagnosis, Jared succumbed to the disease.

Oliver stood by Jared's bedside in the hospital in Mumbai, holding his friend's hand during his final moments. The loss was unbearable. He had watched his once-vibrant, unstoppable friend deteriorate in a matter of months, his life cut short by a disease that, had it been caught earlier, might have been treated. The helplessness Oliver felt deepened his resolve. The experience changed him forever. He vowed to dedicate himself to improving cancer diagnostics, particularly for the early detection of lung cancer, so that others would not have to experience the same heartbreak he had felt watching Jared's life slip away.

With this unfortunate occurrence and in the midst of so much sorrow, Oliver felt his mission taking shape. His experiences and the knowledge gained from mentors like Dr. Shah had fueled his passion for innovation. He realized that his medical and engineering backgrounds could be combined to tackle the problem of late-stage cancer diagnoses and improve surgical precision. Determined to make a difference, Oliver resolved that his final-year project would focus on developing a robotic arm powered by artificial intelligence (AI), capable of performing delicate, intricate surgeries with unparalleled precision. The AI component would also include an algorithm designed to detect early signs of cancer by analyzing patient data, imaging, genetics and clinical patterns that might otherwise go unnoticed by the human eye.

Oliver's vision was clear: a future where cancer could be detected earlier, and surgeries could be performed with robotic precision, drastically improving outcomes and offering new hope to patients who had previously faced insurmountable odds. He was ready to embark on his journey to change the landscape of cancer diagnostics and treatment.

His scholarship at UnGen was structured to allow him to complete this project at one of a few world-leading universities abroad, and he had chosen the Massachusetts Institute of Technology (MIT) in Boston. MIT, with its cutting-edge research facilities and leading experts in robotics and AI, was the ideal environment for Oliver to bring his ambitious vision to life.

Upon arriving at MIT, Oliver was fortunate enough to join Dr. Seff's renowned laboratory, a hub for groundbreaking research in medical robotics and artificial intelligence. Dr. Seff, one of the world's leading experts in this field, quickly recognized the potential in Oliver's proposal.

With the immense support of his research team, Oliver's project was refined to ensure both practicality and scalability for real-world applications. A key focus was making the technology accessible and applicable in low-income countries.

Dr. Seff paired Oliver with Vonne, a postdoctoral researcher whose work intersected significantly with his. Vonne had been working on precision surgical robotics for two years and had developed a deep understanding of both the technical and clinical challenges in this domain. She was not only a gifted mentor but also compassionate and supportive. She began by encouraging Oliver to fully share his vision—and more importantly, the inspiration behind it.

As Oliver recounted the emotional story of his friend Jared, Vonne was deeply moved. The tale of helplessly watching Jared succumb to late-stage cancer resonated with her on a personal level. Vonne had experienced a similar tragedy three years earlier, losing a close friend to cancer in her hometown of Lima, Peru, under eerily similar circumstances. The shared grief over losing loved ones to late diagnoses of cancer forged a powerful connection between them.

"We will form a formidable team," Vonne had said, her voice thick with emotion. "I've been here for two years, learning everything I can to make this technology successful. But what we were missing was exactly what you've brought—a shared purpose and passion to revolutionize cancer treatment."

From that day forward, there was no looking back. Oliver and Vonne worked tirelessly, combining their skills and knowledge to accelerate the project's development. They made rapid progress, refining the AI-powered robotic arm to enhance precision during surgeries, especially in delicate procedures like cancer resections. At the same time, they developed the algorithm capable of analyzing vast amounts of patient data, including genomic, radiological, and clinical information, to detect the earliest signs of cancer—long before symptoms would typically appear.

Before long, Oliver stood at Boston Logan International Airport, bidding an emotional farewell to Vonne and his MIT colleagues. His time in Boston had been transformative, both personally and professionally. The project they had worked on had yielded cutting-edge technology that was poised to revolutionize both cancer diagnostics and surgical interventions, especially in resource-limited settings like his home country of Kenya.

Returning to Nairobi, Oliver arrived as an accomplished innovator, just weeks before the graduation ceremony. During the awards presentation, the chancellor emphasized that his category, consisting of only three individuals, was receiving a degree that had never before been awarded at any University globally, let alone UnGen: Intelligent Surgical Medicine and Diagnostics (ISMD). As Oliver listened to the chancellor's words, pride swelled within him. This degree represented not just his hard work and dedication, but also the future of medicine—a future where technology and healthcare would merge to improve patient outcomes. The ceremony felt like a celebration of innovation and a testament to his journey, igniting a renewed sense of purpose in him as he prepared to make an impact in the field. His mission abroad had borne fruit, and he now carried with him technology that could bridge the gap in cancer care in Kenya and similar regions. His AI-driven innovations were set to drastically improve early cancer detection and enable precision surgeries, even in hospitals lacking advanced medical infrastructure. The future looked promising, and Oliver was ready to lead the charge in transforming cancer care for patients who had previously been left with few options.

His journey had just begun.

But not everyone was pleased. The traditional diagnostic companies and laboratories in Nairobi, where he tested his prototypes, began to take notice. They had been using the same systems for years, raking in profits without innovation. Oliver's work was a direct threat to their business model.

Oliver's breakthroughs in AI diagnostics were nothing short of revolutionary. Unlike traditional methods that required invasive biopsies or expensive machinery, his AI-driven microchips could detect cancer using easily obtainable samples like breath, saliva, tears, hair, and urine. These non-invasive techniques not only made testing more accessible but also eliminated the fear and discomfort often associated with medical procedures.

The process was astonishingly efficient: minute samples were applied to the microchips, and within less than a minute, the AI would determine the presence or absence of specific cancers. What truly set Oliver's diagnostic system apart was its ability to provide real-time, actionable insights. If cancer was detected, the AI instantly recommended the most appropriate, personalized treatment for the individual. It wasn't just a diagnostic tool; it functioned as a precision healthcare advisor. The system could analyze unique patient characteristics—such as gender, age, genetics, environment, and other factors—to select the most effective therapy, offering a highly tailored approach to treatment.

Even more thrilling was the system's ability to assess cancer risks in healthy individuals. The AI could analyze data to identify potential future cancer risks and recommend lifestyle changes or preventative measures long before the disease could develop. This opened up a new frontier in healthcare—one where diseases could be preempted rather than just treated. Oliver's system held the potential to dramatically reduce cancer rates across Africa and beyond, especially if implemented early in life. Childhood cancers, in particular, could be largely kept at bay with early diagnostics, offering hope to millions of families.

And it wasn't just advanced technology—it was accessible. Oliver designed the system to be user-friendly, requiring minimal training to operate. Anyone with basic knowledge of how to use a smartphone could master the diagnostic tool with just 20 minutes of orientation. This ease of use meant that even in rural areas, where healthcare workers were scarce, people could administer life-saving tests with confidence.

As Oliver's AI diagnostics began to gain attention in Nairobi's hospitals, it quickly became apparent that his invention was on the cusp of transforming healthcare. However, not everyone shared the excitement. Traditional diagnostic companies, laboratories, and healthcare providers that had dominated the market for decades were less than thrilled. Oliver's innovation was a direct threat to their established business models, which relied on expensive, time-consuming tests and specialized equipment.

In boardrooms across the city, executives from these companies held frantic meetings, discussing how Oliver's technology would disrupt their monopolies. If anyone could run a cancer test using a portable AI chip and a smartphone, what need would there be for their multimillion-dollar machines? They began to conspire, turning to the one resource they still controlled: policy.

Soon, powerful lobbyists representing these companies pressured policymakers, arguing that Oliver's diagnostics were unproven and risky. They feared his AI might one day replace human doctors altogether, and they warned of "unregulated" technology flooding the market. Behind closed doors, deals were made. Politicians—many of whom had received campaign donations from these industries—agreed to re-evaluate the youth fund grant that had been crucial to Oliver's project. His initiative had been awarded a generous sum, with the health minister highlighting its clear transformative potential.

One morning, Oliver received the news he had dreaded. The email was brief but devastating: due to "re-evaluations" prompted by concerns about the safety and reliability of AI in healthcare, his funding was being cut off prematurely. The very lifeline that had allowed him to develop his diagnostics was severed.

His team was in disbelief. Years of work—thousands of hours spent researching; prototyping, and testing—could vanish in an instant. Without the financial backing to continue, Oliver's project faced potential collapse. Nairobi's startup scene buzzed with rumors of what might happen next. Would Oliver be forced to give up? Would he sell his technology to one of the companies that had been trying to stifle it? Oliver, though shaken, wasn't ready to back down. He was not exactly worried for himself. At least he would continue working at UnGen's affiliated teaching hospital. He knew his AI diagnostics held the key to saving lives. The real challenge wasn't just in innovating; it was in standing up to those who feared change.

As the wise say, "A kind heart is a fountain of gladness." By sheer coincidence, during an evening walk through Jeevanjee Gardens to ponder his predicament, Oliver unexpectedly ran into one of his old high school friends, Javan.

He had heard fast footsteps approaching from behind but hadn't bothered to turn around, assuming it was just another passerby like many before. However, a tap on his shoulder made him pause. To his surprise, it was Javan, another close friend from their high school days.

Javan, now the Human Resource Manager at NeuroSynix PLC, a pioneering AI and robotics company, was thrilled to reconnect. NeuroSynix had gained recognition for revolutionizing medical diagnostics and treatment through advanced, non-invasive technologies that improved precision and accessibility in healthcare. The reunion felt timely, as Javan's new role offered potential opportunities for collaboration that could align perfectly with Oliver's vision for transforming cancer care in resource-limited settings.

NeuroSynix had recently set base at the much-hyped Konza Technopolis. During this chance encounter, Javan introduced Oliver to his companion, Kirov, the CEO of NeuroSynix and a globally renowned AI expert and developer. Kirov had already heard about Oliver's work and instantly recognized its groundbreaking potential. Ironically, the very attempt to bring Oliver down had backfired—his work had been widely publicized, both in print and digital media, by those trying to discredit him. This unwanted attention only served to highlight his brilliance, making his innovations impossible to ignore. After a brief talk, it was agreed that Oliver comes to see Kirov at NeuroSynix early next morning with his prototypes.

"Your ideas are brilliant, but you're ahead of your time. That's why they fear you," Kirov remarked after studying Oliver's prototypes. "But I can help you bring this to the world stage."

Under Kirov's mentorship, Oliver's vision expanded. Kirov connected him with international investors and brought him to global conferences, where his work quickly garnered attention. In no time, Oliver's innovations were receiving global recognition. The same companies that once sought to suppress his progress were now eager to form partnerships with him.

Years later, as Oliver stood on stage, accepting an international award for innovation in medical robotics, he reflected on his journey. From the heartlands of Uasin Gishu, torn between medicine and robotics, to the global stage—his path had been anything but straightforward.

His AI-driven medical robots were now saving lives worldwide, particularly in remote areas where doctors were scarce. Nairobi had become a beacon of medical technology, and Oliver's story was the spark that ignited Africa's leadership in the field.

But for Oliver, this was only the beginning. The future was here, and it was limitless.

The End

# The Necklace of Courage

Odhis was a celebrated fisherman who lived on a tiny, overcrowded island in the middle of Lake Victoria. His home was nestled among many other huts, all crowded together as families relied on the bounty of the lake for their survival. Odhis was no stranger to challenges. He had weathered fierce storms, fought fierce battles, and faced countless uncertainties. Yet through it all, he had always emerged victorious, earning the respect and admiration of everyone who knew him. Many called him "The Lucky One," for fortune always seemed to smile upon him.

But Odhis knew better. His incredible luck stemmed from an event that had happened years ago, an encounter that changed his life.

One day, as Odhis made his routine trip from the island to the Lakeside eateries and further to Kibuye Market to sell his catch, fate had another plan. That was the day he met Farhiya, a shy young girl from the Rendile community. Farhiya had come long ways from her homeland in the Northeastern part of Kenya. Her parent's home was located 46 miles away from the town of Marsabit. Farhiya had come to Lake Victoria in the company of foreign tourists from Rome. While touring the deserts and surrounding communities, tourists greatly benefited from the presence of educated locals in their company, who helped break the language barrier. Antonio, the leader of the tourists, had convinced Farhiya's parents to let her accompany them as a translator in their Kisumu trip in exchange for a generous payment that could fund her education.

At the market, Farhiya found herself in a tricky situation. After enjoying a local dish prepared by Auma, a vendor selling traditional Luo fish cuisine, Antonio wanted to write down the recipe. Although Farhiya spoke fluent Swahili and English, she was completely unfamiliar with Luo. She had never even heard the language spoken before. The challenge was becoming clear: neither Farhiya nor Auma could spell the names of the ingredients in Auma's recipe. Antonio was a meticulous person who took fine details very seriously, which posed a significant problem. He looked to Farhiya for a solution. In his deep voice, with an unmistakable Italian accent, he said, "Just take your time, Farhiya, but I expect you to figure out a way out of this." Farhiya now felt the real heat of her job. Kisumu was hot as expected, but now, it was melting hot. Everyone around was busy, immersed in their own business. Courage—this was the word of the moment. It was the one thing Farhiya needed most yet couldn't summon. I must do something right away, she thought. I need to brave myself and ask someone for help, but who? She agonized, her grandmother's words about the necklace she now graciously adorned flashing through her mind. There was hardly time to ponder.

By coincidence, that's when Odhis arrived, his boat brimming with fresh fish for Auma's stall. As they say, "Face is the index of the mind." When Farhiya set eyes on Odhis, she instinctively knew he was the right person. Seizing the moment, Farhiya asked Odhis for help. Without hesitation, Odhis translated the recipe, carefully spelling out each. But he didn't stop there. He even took the time to explain the preparation process, going above and beyond what was asked of him. Antonio was so impressed that he insisted on giving Odhis a generous tip, a sum far greater than what he would earn from selling his fish that day.

Despite the tempting offer, Odhis was conflicted. He had always believed in earning his keep through hard work, and the thought of accepting such a large tip for something so simple made him uneasy. After much thought, he declined the money. Instead, he suggested something surprising. He asked Farhiya if he could buy her necklace for the price of the tip from Antonio—the beautiful necklace she always wore around her neck.

The necklace was far from ordinary. Although its monetary value was modest, its symbolism was priceless. It had been given to Farhiya by her paternal grandmother, Asha, just before she passed away. In her final moments, Asha had placed the necklace in Farhiya's hands, saying, "I bless you with great fortune and courage, my little one. Wear it, and let my joy be complete as I depart in peace."

Farhiya hesitated. The necklace was immensely precious to her, a cherished gift from her grandmother. But she also realized the potential blessing this exchange could bring. With the money Antonio had offered, she could build her parents a new home, pay school fees for her six siblings, and buy a small herd of camels and goats for her aging father. After thinking it over, she agreed to the deal.

Before parting with the necklace, Farhiya explained its significance to Odhis. "This necklace has given me courage," she said. "Without it, I would never have ventured so far from home." She shared the full story of how she came to possess the necklace, with Odhis listening intently. "I'm naturally very shy, but wearing this necklace has made me brave enough to travel to this city and meet new people," she continued. "Its rightful name is 'The Necklace of Courage.' It's what it is to me. A quick reflection on it emboldened me to talk to you. Are you sure you want to take it from me? Do you understand what happens once I let go of it?"

Odhis thought for a moment. Then, with a smile, he made a suggestion. "How about sharing the necklace?" he proposed. "When I get home, I'll give it to my daughter, Akoth, who is your age. You two can take turns wearing it.

Whenever school is out, you can visit each other, and the necklace will travel between you both. It will be a symbol of your sisterhood, spreading your grandmother's blessings beyond your village and family."

Farhiya smiled at the idea. Growing up with brothers, she had always wished for a sister, and now she had one in Akoth. She handed the necklace to Odhis, knowing it would also bring courage and joy to Akoth as it had to her. Antonio, moved by the exchange, respected Farhiya's wishes and admired the bond being formed.

From that day on, Odhis felt a profound connection to the necklace. He gifted it to Akoth, who wore it proudly. Something unexpected began to happen. It wasn't long before Odhis noticed a change in his own life. He had always been courageous, but now his courage seemed to have multiplied.

One evening, as Odhis sailed his boat across the choppy waters of Lake Victoria, his mind wandered down memory lane. As a young boy, he had always accompanied his father on his fishing expeditions. It was always peaceful and quiet in the deep waters and back home on the tiny island. However, things had changed greatly in recent times. The population had ballooned, putting immense pressure on the limited resources, spurred by the discovery that the tiny island was surrounded by a part of the lake rich in fish resources. Initially, no one really cared about the territorial location of the island, but now, there were two different flags hoisted signifying a deep-rooted contention between nationalities. So deep was this contention that on various occasions, fishermen woke up only to find out that they had lost valuables ranging from their boats, boat engines, and fishing nets. This was consistently blamed on the existing stiff rivalry among individuals from different East African nationalities, mainly Kenya and Uganda.

Odhis had on many occasions felt quite threatened by the thoughts of a possible fight. Not because he was a coward himself, but he mostly feared for his wife and children, especially if there was such an occurrence while he was deep in the waters. But on this day, he felt quite courageous and reassured, and he kept wondering why. On further reflection, he remembered the sudden change he had noticed in his daughter Akoth. Her confidence and courage had risen to unbelievable levels. She had become a beacon of hope and strength, not just for the family, but for the entire community. He thought about Akoth's poem, which she had recited during a recent Chief's meeting to discuss peace on the island. The poem was powerful and sobering, with the theme: "there is always enough for all; fighting is not necessary."

The four-line chorus of Akoth's poem went as follows:

*We share this earth, a vast and boundless place,*
*Where every soul deserves a sacred space.*
*In unity, we rise, with hearts that never fall,*
*Hand in hand, we thrive—one world, one call.*

That Akoth could do this was unexpected. Reflecting on himself, he realized how much his own courage had grown. For some time, certain decisions had been left unmade, all for the same reason: a lack of courage to face the consequences. But recently, that hesitation had vanished. His focus had shifted to simply doing the right thing, no matter what. He had learned that with this approach, he could never go wrong. "What incredible fortune I've found!" he marveled. "That necklace is truly phenomenal!"

Odhis had been so deeply absorbed in his thoughts that he did not notice the brewing storm. Before he could consider his short list of available options for an action plan, the storm suddenly hit. The waves were taller than he had ever seen, and for the first time in years, Odhis felt fear creep into his heart. His boat was being tossed like a leaf in the wind, and the sky had turned as dark as night. As the storm raged, he gripped the tiller tightly, his thoughts turning to the Necklace of Courage around his daughter Akoth's neck. He remembered her stories of bravery, amazed at how simply reflecting on the necklace's significance filled him with newfound strength. Though the necklace was with Akoth, its magic seemed to reach him across the distance. Drawing on their shared courage, Odhis steered the boat through the storm with renewed determination, battling the fierce winds and waves toward safety.

As the storm subsided, Odhis realized he had survived something that might have otherwise claimed his life. The necklace had worked its magic yet again, giving him the courage to face the fury of the lake. This became just one of the many instances when the magic of the necklace of courage had come in very handy for Odhis.

Another time, Odhis was confronted by a group of fishermen from across the borders. They had made claims that Odhis had ventured beyond the boundary and was now fishing in their waters, a claim which even the border control unit later confirmed was far from the truth. These fishermen were known to be aggressive and did not hesitate to use force to take what they wanted. Odhis knew that standing up to them would be dangerous. Armed with only his courage and the thought of his family, Odhis stood his ground. He calmly negotiated with the rival fishermen, explaining the long-standing traditions of the island and its people. The situation grew tense, but Odhis remained resolute. His voice did not waver, and his eyes did not show fear. In the end, the rival fishermen backed down, impressed by his courage and conviction.

To this day, the necklace of courage remains a cherished symbol of the bond between Farhiya and Akoth. Though they live far apart, their sisterhood endures, strengthened by their shared courage and the blessings of their ancestors.

And as for Odhis, he continues to navigate the challenges of life on the island with the same courage that has always seen him through—knowing that, no matter what, the necklace of courage is always close by, a reminder of the strength that lies within him.

The End

# A Journey to the Kenyan Skies and Beyond

Komen, now an accomplished middle-distance runner, often found himself gazing out of the plane window, marveling at the clouds that stretched endlessly beneath him. His journey to the skies was far more than a literal ascent—it was a journey that had started long before he had even set sight on a plane.

Born in the remote village of Chepkorio, nestled in the slopes of Elgeiyo, Komen grew up with his family of nine. As the firstborn son, life demanded much from him. The absence of his father, Chelimo, who was often away in search of greener pastures for his cattle, left Komen in charge of responsibilities far beyond his age. His mother, Chebaibai, was a strong woman, but with so many young children to care for, she leaned heavily on Komen to fill the gaps left by his father. As years went by, Komen grew up both in stature and experience. The experience came at a premium obviously as his mother heavily relied on him to handle multiple tasks. Sometime he felt that nature was on a conspiracy mission against him. As a first born boy, many heavy duties in the family rested on his shoulders - at the slopes chores were clearly segregated, with the track towards manhood being heavily lined up with tough roles.

Komen's life was one of endurance. He would wake before dawn, taking the sheep and goats out to graze, and trek the two miles to the river to fetch water. Balancing two twenty-liter jerricans over his shoulders, he would climb the steep paths home, his legs growing stronger with each trip. Yet even after this laborious morning routine, his work was far from over. He would then help his younger siblings get ready for the long trek to Kapkoros Primary School, where they would many times arrive just minutes after the assembly bell had rung—often resulting in punishment for their lateness. Because of the long distance between home and school, lunch was rarely an option for Komen and his siblings, except during the green maize season when they each carried a cob in their school bags. For the rest of the year, they would walk to the river a mile away to quench their thirst, joining a few other children from the village. The other students, who lived closer to school, would rush home for lunch and return before the 2 o'clock bell. Komen and his siblings would then have to endure the lively conversations of their classmates, who often discussed what they had for lunch. To Komen, it always felt like a test of patience, as if they deliberately wanted him to listen and feel envious.

He vividly remembered the day he received a harsh beating from his mother, Chebaibai, for accepting a lunch invitation from a friend whose home was a cross the fence from school. Overcome by hunger, he had broken one of the family's strict rules: not one of them was allowed to eat by themselves. This meant that at the very least, he should have taken the entire group of siblings to his friend's home or brought back something for them. When Komen returned to school with a full stomach, his siblings were not amused. Worse still, he had failed to take them to the river, leaving them hungry, thirsty, and angry. His immediate younger sister, now second in command and particularly frustrated by the others' complaints while their team leader, Komen was away, wasted no time in reporting the incident to their mother, when they arrived home later that evening. And of course, Chebaibai swiftly delivered what she considered as instant and befitting justice.

The walk home was always much faster, as delays carried dire consequences—whether it meant sleeping on damp bedding after evening rains or going to bed hungry. Komen knew life did not afford him any room for negotiation. In fact, he believed he was already getting the best of what was possible under the prevailing circumstances. Hard work and endurance were etched into his spirit, and he faced life's challenges with quiet acceptance and determination. While at home, he never rested until everyone's needs were met, except his mother's some of which were beyond him. Sometimes, he stayed up a little longer to attempt his school homework, while his exhausted mother sat quietly beside him. Occasionally, she would interrupt to ask if he had checked that all the goats were safely home or if he had secured the poultry house properly. Their neighbor's dog had become quite skilled at breaching the locking system, forcing her to make frequent adjustments.

When the kerosene lantern finally dimmed, Komen would instantly collapse into a deep sleep, oblivious to the hard ground beneath him with a goat skin as the only intervention in between. The blanket from KENIT factory in Eldoret had seen better days. Only three such were available to be shared by eight of the siblings, with little Lily the lastborn getting to share in mum's. For this family members, like everyone else in their village, a mattress was something they would rarely encounter. Sleeping on goat skins was the norm, and no one could imagine anything different.

Though Komen's days were filled with hardship, his nights offered an escape. Fortunately, as soon as Komen closed his eyes, he was always transported to dreamland, where the burdens of the day melted away.

He had always been fascinated by the planes that occasionally flew over his home, though he regretted they were too high in the sky for him to get a clear view. In his dreams, however, he was no longer the overburdened boy of Chepkorio; he was free. He soared above the vast Kenyan landscape, gliding effortlessly through the skies.

The rolling hills, the Great Rift Valley, and the golden savannahs of the Maasai Mara—all passed beneath him with ease. No longer weighed down by daily chores, he ruled the skies, an adventurer in his own right.

His dreams, however, were more than just flights of fancy. They gave him a sense of hope, a belief that there was more to life than the small village in which he lived. The dreams painted a picture of a world far beyond what he knew, and though he had never seen the inside of an airplane, he felt as though he was destined to experience more.

It was on a visit to his Aunt's house in Iten that Komen first caught a clear glimpse of an airplane. On the small TV screen, a news broadcast showed the landing of a plane, its passengers disembarking with their luggage. Komen's heart raced as he watched, captivated by the sight. The idea of flying felt like something from another world, reserved for the wealthy and fortunate—categories he never imagined himself part of. Yet, despite this, a spark of ambition ignited within him.

Life continued as it always had, but now a small flame of desire began to flicker in Komen's heart. He didn't know how or when, but he yearned to break free from the confines of his daily routine and reach for something higher. Little did he realize that every morning run to school, every uphill trek carrying water, every dash to fetch goats and sheep from the fields was silently preparing him for something far greater.

Komen's natural athleticism evolved alongside his growing sense of duty. Running had become second nature to him, his long, steady strides leading his siblings to school daily. While admired by his peers, Komen rarely paid attention to their praise. Running was simply a part of life—a means to survive, not something to be celebrated.

That all changed during a local event commemorating an internationally renowned marathon legend, whose promising career had been tragically cut short by a car accident. It was here that Komen caught the eye of a local teacher, who noticed his effortless speed. "Have you ever considered running competitively?" the teacher asked.

The idea had never occurred to Komen. Running was just a necessity, something woven into the fabric of his everyday life. But the teacher's words planted a seed. He realized that, though he had raced against time and chores, he had never raced on an official track. In fact, there was hardly anything resembling a track at Kapkoros Primary School.

The second term was usually reserved for athletics, and races would start at 4:00 p.m. after all classes had ended. Participation was optional, and only those with the inclination would stay. The older boys would mark out lanes on the field with used engine oil, but keeping the lines straight was almost impossible. Still, they served their purpose.

When the 4:00 p.m. bell rang, for Komen, it signaled something far more urgent than racing: the need to gather his siblings and lead them home. Racing, to him, wasn't a luxury; it was survival. His competitive streak, however, thrived in other ways. When fetching water at the river, Komen would challenge his peers to carry their jerricans uphill without stopping. He won nearly every contest, except one against his younger sister, Chebet, who had only carried one small can on that occasion. Komen had given her a head start and by bad luck tripped at the beginning. In his trip, he ensured that not a single drop of water was spilled. His mother, Chebaibai, had watched from afar and later warned him, 'There's no glory in racing those you're sure to beat. Find your match.

At school, Komen saw no need to compete, with peers as he was certain of victory. Interestingly, when the 4:00 p.m. bell rang, his classmates would urge him to head home quickly, knowing they stood no chance if he stayed for the evening races. As the saying goes "Good advice from a friend can sometimes disguise selfish intentions". But on that fateful day of honoring the marathon legend, Komen did something unexpected—even surprising himself.

Kapkoros Primary School had failed to register anyone for the 1500-meter race—the ultimate test of speed and endurance. Not wanting to see his school embarrassed, Komen stepped forward. e didn't expect to win. Confused by the idea of running 1500 meters, he had sought advice from the school games teacher, unsure even of how many laps it entailed. The distance seemed abstract to his naïve mind. As he stood at the starting line, he noticed some of the runners wore shoes—something Komen had never seen. He muttered aloud, "What are those for?" To him, shoes seemed like a burden.

The race began, and Komen found himself among the leading pack by the second lap. At the end of the third lap, when the bell rang to signal the final stretch, Komen was unsure if his competitors were conserving their energy for the last 100 meters. That is how it appeared to him. For a moment, he was tempted to do the same, but then realized he felt just as fresh as when he started. Yet his muscles had now warmed up, and his legs were ready for more. Without hesitation, he began his sprint 300 meters before the finish line.

Two runners, Biwott and Tarus, attempted to keep pace but soon fell behind. Komen crossed the finish line nearly 10 meters ahead of Biwott, a revered figure who had represented the county at the national level countless times. Three years older and already in high school, Biwott was expected to represent the region in the upcoming East African Secondary Schools Championships in Nambole, Uganda. When Biwott came over to shake Komen's hand, the crowd erupted in cheers, but it was the look of respect in Biwott's eyes that caught Komen off guard. Respect was the last thing Komen expected. As he stepped off the track and reached for his torn shirt—having run the race bare-chested—his schoolmates lifted him onto their shoulders. Even the girls who had teased him for years, mocking him for wearing the same clothes and smelling of sweat, suddenly threw their arms around him in congratulations.

As a chronic daydreamer, he had to pinch himself to believe it wasn't just another fantasy. Soon after that race, Komen's journey as a competitive runner began. His raw talent shone through, and local races became his proving ground, with each step taking him closer to a future he had never imagined.

As Komen's talent blossomed, so did his opportunities. He was selected to represent his school at regional events, where he outran competitors with a lot more athletic experience than he did. In the meantime he quickly progressed through the ranks and it was soon time to sit his final year examinations.

Komen didn't perform well in his end-of-primary school exams—the Kenya Certificate of Primary Examinations. No one was surprised, least of all Komen, as his marks mirrored what he had consistently scored throughout his final year at Kapkoros. He hadn't had much time to prepare, often constrained for time or too tired to read or do his homework. Much to his delight and surprise, several schools came calling at his rural home, seeking to admit him. He was even more surprised when they offered him full scholarships. One Saturday morning in December stood out: three school coaches—one each from St. Patricks Iten, Paul Boit, and St. Joseph Boys—converged at his home.

Chelimo, who had just arrived the previous evening from the fields, was in shock when he stepped out of his round, grass-thatched hut that morning. His immediate thought was to run away. He looked carefully at the three parked vehicles and, seeing no signs of police uniforms or guns, decided to stay. The coach from Iten read his mind and spoke first: "We have come in peace," he said. "We have no intention of taking much of your valuable time. If you allow us, we can have a brief conversation with your son, Komen."

Chelimo's shock deepened. How did they know his little boy's name? To him, people riding in vehicles weren't supposed to know anyone from his house hold, not even himself. He wondered if Komen was capable of committing any crimes. "Why are you here?" he almost shouted. "I have no local brew in my house. My wife stopped making it almost a decade ago. My son Komen is only a child. Why would you be looking for him?"

“It’s alright, it’s all good, baba Komen,” said Lawrence, the coach from Paul Boit School. "You have an amazing child. Look, we didn’t plan on converging here—meaning the three of them—as he pointed at the other eminent coaches. But your son is a magnet. He has magically drawn us to your house today. We are all seeking to admit him to our respective schools. Interestingly, all three schools are offering him full scholarships. That means he won’t pay a cent for the four years of secondary school education. I’m afraid you’ll have trouble deciding where to let him go. If you would listen to me, I plead he joins..."

“Wait a minute,” interrupted Titus, the head coach from St. Patricks Iten High School. "Let’s all place our offers on the table and let Komen and his parents decide." Chelimo could hardly believe his ears. He was seen several times pushing his fingers into his ears and rubbing them gently as if to clean them for better hearing. He asked the guests to hold their horses briefly as he instructed Komen and Chebet to bring out wooden stools and arrange them under a tree shade next to the goat house. "It is not our norm to entertain our guests while they stand like sugarcane. We have to sit under the shade and at the very least start with formal introductions. You’re only fortunate that I arrived last night from my many months away to cater for my herd of cattle. My wife would have sent you away pending my arrival—which usually is indeterminate." Meanwhile, he pulled Chebet aside and whispered something into her ear.

As they settled down, Chebaibai arrived, carrying a long guard filled with fresh milk. "Again, you’re very fortunate,” he said. “The herds are around, and you can drink your fill.” He then asked Komen to serve the guests. "After all, these are your guests," he said.

Soon, it was time for introductions. The guests spent the next hour convincing Chelimo that Komen was a very good runner. "You’ve come all this way to tell me about the abilities of a child that I’ve raised with my own hands! You don’t feel weird describing the qualities of a son to his own father, rather than letting him (the father) do the talking?" he joked.

Titus pulled out his smartphone and asked to show Chelimo something. It was a clip of Komen doing the last lap during the event to celebrate the departed marathoner. Chelimo was in awe. "That is my son," he repeated several times. Going forward, he needed no further convincing. He sat very alert to hear what the coaches had to say next.

They all did their best at pitching their schools, hoping to win Chelimo's favor and get his son to join their institutions. They had expected a very engaging discussion based on the details of their offers, but—shock on them—all Chelimo wanted to know was how far their schools were from his home. So, as it turned out, St. Patrick Iten Boys High School being the closest carried the day. For Komen, the outcome didn't matter much. He had been worried that he might never set foot in high school. He had been concerned about two things: whether his dad would consider spending any family resources on 'costly high school education', and whether his mother would be willing to let him go, given her dependence on him. The scholarship easily resolved the first concern. St. Patricks was letting Komen walk into the school like he had arrived in this world at birth—empty- handed. They would go beyond paying school fees to taking care of all the requirements, including uniform, beddings, and books. The school even offered to provide pocket money to cover travel expenses and other out-of- pocket costs. Once this was fully explained, Chelimo cleared his throat and spoke in a calm yet piercing tone.

"You've heard that I arrived last night after many months of absence from this homestead. I am convinced you all know who might have been taking care of my wife in my absence." The coaches all lifted their heads in synchrony as though on remote control. "Do I need to explain any further, or is my point driven home already?" Titus searched quickly and deeply through his options. "One of the board members, who happen to be a leading supporter of sporting talent at our school, lives about 2 km up the street. He has a vast chunk of land with luxuriant grazing meadow. From what I see, your herd is quite small. I will converse with him so you don't have to travel far to find pastures. You can spend time around your family, and Chebaibai will be really pleased."

Chelimo couldn't hide his joy at the news. "You will allow me at least one month so I can get my son Komen through the rites to become a man. One of the reasons I traveled all this way is to make this happen. The ceremony will be the day after tomorrow, and we have called in relatives from afar to join us on this auspicious occasion. You are all welcome to attend," he said. Being from within, they all understood the undertakings required. Komen was going through the rite of circumcision, which was held in high regard among the Keiyo people. School was not starting till mid-January, so the deal was perfect.

Although the other two coaches were not successful, they appeared content with the offer given to Komen. Komen's humility quickly won all of them over to the extent that all they now wanted was the best for him. Their goodwill touched Chelimo's heart. "To you, Titus, you have carried the day. I have fully agreed to your bid and can't wait to allow my son to come to your school. So, you have fully received the reward of the day. And to you, Benard and Laurence, I owe you a lot of gratitude for considering my son, even though things haven't gone your way. As is our custom, you shall not leave empty-handed," he said, before hurrying off. He soon returned, dragging two young he-goats. "This is my way of thanking you and apologizing for not accepting your generous offers. There are many other little Komens in the community. I wish you luck in finding them. As they say, all's well that ends well." With that, the coaches set out to leave.

Komen sat down under the huge tree, skimming through his Form 1 admission letter from Titus. "I thank you, my good Lord," he said gazing into the blue sky. "I have heard and read about your miracles— yet this very day, as you would have it, one is unfolding before my eyes, and I happen to be the lead character in it."

When January finally came, Komen was all set. He reported to school filled with gratitude and determination in his heart and mind.

He promised himself that he would at least get the two most important missions right, as far as it depended on him: education and athletic excellence. And this he did. The more he raced, the more attention he garnered, until one day, after participating in the National Secondary School Championships, a scout from the Kenyan Athletics Federation approached him.

"We'd like you to come and train at our Iten high altitude training centre," the scout said, his eyes gleaming with the recognition of raw talent. "You have the potential to go far, Komen. I mean very far."

The words felt surreal, as though they belonged to someone else. But soon enough, Komen found himself training at one of the most renowned high-altitude camps in the world, surrounded by elite athletes. It was there that he learned discipline, strategy, and the art of middle-distance running. The very same hills that had once been the source of his struggle now became his training grounds.

Komen's first international race came sooner than he could have imagined. As he stepped off the plane in Europe, the dream he had once lived only in his sleep now became reality. The airplane cabin felt strangely familiar, though this time, it wasn't a dream—he was truly flying. The young boy from Elgeiyo had made it to the skies, and beyond.

With each race, Komen's name became known around the world. He traveled from continent to continent, always taking a moment during his flights to gaze out at the skies he once ruled only in his dreams. Now, he was not just a passenger, but a conqueror of both the track and the skies.

His success on the track brought him wealth and recognition, but Komen never forgot where he came from. He returned to Chepkorio often, visiting his mother and siblings, always bringing something to make their lives easier. The family rule always lingered: no one was allowed to eat alone. The heavy burdens of his childhood had shaped him into the man he had become—strong, determined, and unshakable.

Though Komen had reached the heights he once only dreamed of, he was not content to stop there. His next dream was to give back, to inspire the next generation of young athletes from villages like his own. He established a running camp in his hometown of Chepkorio, training young boys and girls who, like him, carried dreams too big for the ground beneath them.

As he stood watching the young athletes train, Komen knew that their paths, like his, would take them to places far beyond the hills of Elgeiyo. And as they ran, they, too, would soar toward the skies—toward their own futures, limitless and bright.

The end

# Kabosie and the Secrets of the Yala River

Kabosie was only three years old when her father, first brought her to the shores of the mighty Yala River. To her father, the river held deep significance—its waters flowed through the memories of his childhood. His days were spent tending to his father's herd of cattle, sheep, and goats, with the Yala River as his constant companion. He quenched his thirst here, fished in its depths, bathed in its waters, and floated on deadwood logs from the surrounding thick forest. Every one of his elder children in the family had shared multiple of these riverside moments with him, and now it was Kabosie's turn, for the very first time.

All of Kabosie's siblings had displayed their unique brilliance, each in their own distinct way. Igen, the eldest, was on the cusp of finishing primary school and often boasted confidently about securing a spot in one of the top national high schools. During the weekdays, he would dream aloud of attending the prestigious Bush School in Kiambu, but come the weekend, his imagination wandered to the towering boys' school nestled in the heart of Nandi. His younger brother, Ropi, equally gifted, shared similar aspirations but sought a path that set him apart from Igen. Kabosie, as expected, was different from her siblings—quieter, more introspective, and content with her own curious world. She was much quieter and preferred the company of familiar faces—her parents, older siblings, and her beloved nanny, whom she affectionately called Senge. Even at a young age, her inquisitive nature was undeniable. While other children were content playing in the sand or skipping stones across the water, Kabosie's curiosity set her apart. She was always searching for something deeper, something hidden beneath the surface of the ordinary. As she sat beside her father, her small hand gently resting in his, she became transfixed by something in the river.

A towering boulder, rising from the heart of the water, captured her attention. Her eyes locked on it, unblinking, for nearly an hour.

Her father, distracted by his own thoughts, didn't think much of it at first. He had taken her to the river in hopes that it would calm her grumpy mood after she had insisted on following her mother, Kwecho to the market earlier that day. Even the promise of sesame rolls or her favorite roasted fish couldn't lift her spirits. Kabosii's father had hoped that the peaceful riverbanks might work their magic, yet to his surprise, even the smooth stones he'd gathered for her to toss held no appeal. Instead, her gaze never wavered from the mysterious boulder in the middle of the river.

“Isn’t it time to go home?” her father finally asked, noticing the dark clouds gathering overhead. But Kabosie refused to budge, her eyes glued to the rock. With gentle persistence, her father coaxed her to leave, and as they began their ascent up the hill, Kabosie continuously looked back over her shoulder, her little face clouded with awe. Her father, growing worried, even told her the biblical tale of Lot's wife, hoping it would make her stop turning around, but Kabosie seemed lost in her own world.

That night, after returning home, Kabosie sat at her small desk, scribbling furiously in her notebook. The shapes and patterns she drew made no sense to anyone, not even to her beloved nanny, Senge who had always understood her best. Yet Kabosie was undeterred—something about that rock in the river had unlocked a deeper mystery in her mind, and she was determined to uncover it.

Kabosie's father frowned as he picked up her new drawing book, eyeing the scribbles on the first page. His disappointment was evident as he realized she had used the pristine book her mother had brought earlier from the market. "This is meant for serious things, Kabosie," he said, shaking his head slightly. "Your teacher will not be pleased with this mess. You should be drawing proper pictures or practicing your letters, not filling the pages with... whatever this is." He sighed deeply, clearly expecting more from his usually thoughtful daughter, not realizing the depth hidden in her seemingly chaotic lines.

Several weeks later, a traveler arrived in the village—an old magician from Loliondo, Tanzania, renowned for his wisdom and mystical insight. Word had spread of a girl with a strange connection to the Yala River, and it was this rumor that had drawn the magician across borders. Kabosie, since her first encounter at the river, had insisted on accompanying anyone who ventured near it. Her newfound obsession had sparked widespread curiosity in the village, yet no one could pinpoint the exact reason for her deep affinity. When the magician finally laid eyes on Kabosie’s mysterious drawings, his expression shifted.

His eyes widened in recognition, as if he had stumbled upon something profound, hidden in plain sight. "These are no ordinary sketches," he murmured. "These are autostereograms—hidden images that carry deeper meanings. They are ancient, passed down through generations, and only those who can see beyond the surface can unravel their secrets."

Intrigued, Kabosie's father listened as the magician explained how these images, hidden within the landscape of the river, were created by the ancient people who once lived along its banks. They had woven their knowledge into the rocks and waters, waiting for the right person to discover it.

The next morning, the magician took Kabosie and her father back to the Yala River. He pointed to the same boulder that had so mesmerized Kabosie and, with a wave of his hand, revealed the first autostereogram—hidden patterns etched into the stone. As they gazed intently, the swirling lines of the rock began to shift and transform, revealing a map embedded within its surface.

This map led them to another two specific points along the river where the magician showed them the second and third autostereograms. Each one held a different secret.

The first autostereogram unveiled an ancient secret about the Yala River's flow and its vital role in the land's sustenance. It depicted how, upon reaching Lake Victoria, the water droplets would mysteriously sort themselves—those that had joined near the river's source, weary from the long journey, would rest lazily in the lake. Meanwhile, the more energetic droplets, having joined downstream, would gather and prepare for the long, arduous voyage down the Nile to Egypt. "Water has no enemies," the magician said, invoking an old African proverb, reminding everyone of the river's enduring power to connect people across vast distances and nurture life, uniting them in ways beyond mere geography. The second autostereogram was a lesson in balance, revealing how the flow of the Yala River sustained not just the land, but the entire ecosystem. The river nourished the plants, animals, and people in perfect harmony. The villagers had forgotten this balance over generations, but now, with this rediscovery, they could restore it. The magician shared another proverb: "If you want to go fast, go alone. If you want to go far, go together," emphasizing the unity that would be required to preserve the river for future generations.

But it was the third autostereogram that held the most profound secret of all. As Kabosie stared at the intricate patterns, they slowly shifted, forming the outline of a figure—a figure that looked remarkably like her. The message was clear: Kabosie was destined to be the guardian of the river's secrets, a protector who would ensure that the waters continued to flow, sustaining life for years to come. With the magician's guidance, Kabosie shared the knowledge she had unlocked with the village.

One early morning, Kabosie woke up to intense pain on her left rib, so severe that she screamed uncontrollably. Her bewildered parents ran around, unsure of how to help. As the pain intensified, Kabosie suddenly stood up and headed for the door. No one stopped her. She walked in the direction of the Yala River, her cries growing louder with each step. Her father followed closely behind, sensing the deep connection between the river and Kabosie.

Without hesitation, she moved toward the second autostereogram. The moment her eyes locked onto it, the wailing ceased. Kabosie stared intensely at the image, as if decoding a hidden message. She stood transfixed for nearly fifteen minutes. Then, she began speaking, her words unclear at first—much like "speaking in tongues." As her voice softened, her words became crystal clear.

"It is happening soon," she proclaimed. "The river will be stabbed in her ribs very soon. She will bleed, and it cannot be reversed or stopped. But listen—though you cannot stop the bleeding, you can tap the blood. This must happen. Organize and mobilize the people!"

With that, she turned and made her way back home. Her father's house stood on an elevated hill, offering a clear view of the village below, including the home of the village elder. Most of the villagers had already gathered, eagerly awaiting Kabosie's return, now widely respecting her for her powers and deep connection to the river. Just a few weeks earlier, her cries would have been ignored. But after the visit of the Loliondo magician, Kabosie had gained a reputation—a celebrity, even. A mere sneeze from her now drew concern and questions.

As she approached the crowd, she appeared calm, but there was urgency in her eyes. She wasted no time with pleasantries. "Hear me, good people," she announced. "I have seen the river bleed. It will happen soon. Some will drive a great spear into her ribs and take her blood. Be cautious—you may not be able to stop them, but you must demand compensation. The village and the entire community must be compensated. I am only a messenger, the rest is up to you."

As Kabosie walked toward the breakfast table at her father's house, the village elder rose to address the crowd. "We cannot doubt the accuracy of her vision. We can only seek understanding and prepare. We must be wise in interpreting her message."

While the elder was still speaking, a cloud of brown dust rose from the village road. The road, unpaved and dry, sent plumes of dust swirling into the air as three vehicles sped toward the river. The entire village watched, then chased after them, suspecting this was connected to Kabosie's warning.

At the river, nearly ten people emerged from the vehicles. One introduced himself as the regional engineer from the Lake Victoria Water Company. "As you know, water is a national resource," he began. "We are here to explore the possibility of tapping the river to supply clean water to the city. If successful, we'll build a dam, dig trenches, and lay pipes to channel water from here to the city. A treatment plant will also be constructed at the nearby market."

The villagers marveled at the accuracy of Kabosie's vision. Following her guidance, the village elder made it clear they would not oppose the project. "However," he added, "we will require compensation. We ask for nothing more than to be connected to clean water from the treatment plant."

The engineer agreed to the request but asked for time to consult with his company. The elder assured him they would wait, but he made it clear that the village expected a positive response. Kabosie, now finished with her breakfast, nodded approvingly. The crowd watched her with awe and respect.

Three months later, the entire village had access to clean, piped water in their homes—plenty for both domestic use and farming. The community began treating the Yala River, which rises in the Nandi Escarpment in Kenya's Rift Valley, with newfound reverence. They planted trees along its banks, conserved its waters, and protected the delicate balance that had been restored.

And so, the Yala River continued its journey, carrying not just water, but the wisdom of the ages, flowing from the heart of Kenya all the way to Egypt. Kabosie, now recognized as the guardian of the river, watched over it, ensuring that its secrets would be passed down through generations, just as the ancient people had intended.

From that day on, Kabosie was no longer just a little girl captivated by a rock in the river. She had become a protector of life itself, ensuring the river's flow continued, bringing life, wisdom, and magic to all who lived along its mighty banks.

The end.

# Safari Adventure with the Lionhearted Princess of Nandiland

Once upon a time, in the lush and mystical rural country of Nandiland, there lived a radiant and brave young girl named Tasha. She was no ordinary girl, for she was the heir to the throne of Nandiland, descended from the legendary Orgoiyot, Kipnyolei. The royal family, though quiet and secluded, was favored by the great Creator, Asis. Tasha had inherited not only the beauty and grace of her ancestors but also their indomitable courage.

Tasha's life in Cheptol village was filled with joy and laughter, thanks to her loyal friend, Lady Natasha Chebaibai. Natasha was a comedian at heart, always quick with a joke to lighten any situation. Together with their adventurous companions, Jack, Roy, and their trusted driver Keter, they were always ready for excitement. Today, their destination was none other than the famous Maasai Mara, a place where nature's raw beauty and danger met.

As dawn broke, the group set out in their powerful Toyota Land Cruiser, excitement bubbling as they embarked on the safari of a lifetime. The early morning air was crisp, and as they drove through the vast Kenyan plains, they couldn't help but feel a sense of awe at the wilderness around them. However, the road to

adventure is often paved with unexpected challenges.

Just after entering the Mara, the group's conversation shifted to how technology had simplified many aspects of life. Payments, for instance, were now fully cashless—unlike during their previous visits. Park fees were now processed through a government MPESA paybill number, 222222. Keter couldn't help but voice his hope that the money would actually reach the park to support its operations. As their chatter gradually faded, absorbed by the breathtaking landscape of the Mara, a sudden loud bang shattered the peaceful moment. The Land Cruiser swerved sharply to a stop, just meters away from a pride of hungry lions. Panic set in as they watched the majestic beasts eyeing them from a distance. Tasha, however, remained calm, her courage shining through. "Stay still, and don't make any sudden movements," she whispered. While Natasha tried to keep everyone's spirits up with her jokes, Tasha's love for car racing came in handy as she quickly changed the tire, her hands working with lightning speed. Within minutes, they were back on the road, narrowly escaping the hungry lions.

As night descended, they finally reached their campsite, only to be greeted by an unexpected disaster—the entire area was flooded. The weather, which had been forecasted to be warm with a picturesque sunset, had turned into a cold, rainy mess. They had envisioned watching animals gather at the waterhole for their last drink of the day, but now, drenched and shivering, that dream was gone. Tasha's group slogged through the thick mud, trying to find a dry spot for their tents, only to discover that the best areas had already been claimed.

Keter, ever practical, suggested the only option: Tasha and Natasha would sleep inside the Land Cruiser, while the men would sleep on the roof. "We'll keep the torches on to scare away any wildlife," Keter said, trying to reassure them. But by 2:00 a.m., the batteries had died, and darkness engulfed them. The eerie sound of hyenas cackling filled the air. Soon, the number of hyenas grew, and their menacing eyes gleamed as they circled the vehicle, drawn by the scent of potential prey.

As if things couldn't get worse, the hyenas' noise attracted a nearby pride of lions. "Get in, quickly!" Keter shouted as the men scrambled down from the roof. Tasha, woken by the commotion, swiftly unlocked the doors, saving her companions from the encroaching danger.

The next day, the real adventure began. As they journeyed deeper into the Mara, they spotted a two poachers, armed and dangerous. To their horror, the poachers were targeting one of the last remaining white rhinos, a sacred creature protected by Asis himself. Tasha's heart raced as she watched the poachers position themselves, ready to fire. "We can't just sit here and do nothing!" she exclaimed, her voice trembling with anger.

"We'll be killed if we try to stop them," Keter warned. "There's nothing we can do."

But Tasha refused to believe it. "Asis won't let this happen," she whispered, her faith unwavering. Natasha, in her usual lighthearted manner, joked about Asis sending lightning bolts to stop the poachers. Just as the others began to laugh, something extraordinary happened. The lead poacher, just about to pull the trigger, was suddenly flung into the air.

The group watched in disbelief as a massive python, known as Mosee, emerged from the tall grass. Mosee, the legendary protector of the Mara, had wrapped himself around the poachers, tossing them about as if they were rag dolls. Tasha's elation at seeing the rhino spared was swiftly overshadowed by concern for the poachers. Despite their cruel intentions, they were still human, and the thought of them being devoured by Mosee filled her with unease. Tasha couldn't stand by and watch them suffer, no matter their wrongdoing.

Driven by an inner force, Tasha leaped from the Land Cruiser, rushing toward the scene. "Tasha, no!" Keter called after her, but she was already too far gone. The others watched in horror as she ran straight toward the deadly snake. Keter muttered under his breath, "We've lost her."

But Tasha had no fear. She reached into her pocket and pulled out a small bottle of body lotion. With quick thinking, she poured the lotion over Mosee, the slick substance loosening the snake's grip on the poachers. With a final squeeze, the python released them, tossing the terrified men onto the roof of the fast-approaching Land Cruiser, where Natasha had taken control of the wheel.

Mosee turned his gaze to Tasha, their eyes locking for what seemed like an eternity. Then, as if in recognition of her bravery, the mighty python slithered away into the thick brush. As the dust settled, the poachers, shaken and covered in mud, fell to their knees, begging for mercy. "We will never harm another creature again," they cried, tears streaming down their faces.

At that moment, Ole, the lead park ranger, emerged from the trees, his weapon hanging loosely at his side. He recounted how his team had been overpowered by the poachers, forcing them to flee. But now, thanks to Tasha's bravery, the rhino was safe, and justice had been served. Ole swiftly disarmed the poachers and commanded them into submission. "You're fortunate;" he said sternly, "the park is observing a week of peace in honor of the great elephant Lucy, who just gave birth to twins. During this period, I have the authority to grant a prerogative of mercy," Ole continued. "I hereby pardon you, but you will be placed under strict surveillance for the next five years. During this time, you must dedicate yourselves to defending and protecting our fragile ecosystem." The poachers, humbled and relieved, agreed without hesitation and immediately began their new roles as guardians of the land.

From that day forward, the story of Princess Tasha's bravery spread far and wide. The guardians of the jungle, the skies, the rivers, and even the ocean came together in agreement: Tasha, the Lionhearted Princess of Nandiland, had earned the greatest honor ever bestowed upon a human. Her courage, compassion, and quick thinking had saved not only the sacred rhino but also the souls of two men who would go on to become defenders of the wild.

And so, Tasha's name was etched into the annals of history, not just as a princess, but as a true protector of the land, the animals, and the people. Asis, watching from the heavens, smiled upon her, knowing that the future of Nandiland was in the hands of the bravest heart he had ever seen.

The end, or perhaps, just the beginning of Tasha's legendary adventures.

The end

# A Johannesburg Adventure: Dr. Jeff' Fellowship and Family Escapade

Dr. Jeff, a senior faculty member at Moi University in Eldoret had just received an invitation to take up a writing fellowship at the prestigious Johannesburg Institute for Advanced Study (JIAS) in South Africa. The excitement was overwhelming. He had applied for the fellowship after spotting an advertisement sometime back and had been looking forward to a feedback. The moment he opened the email, he held his breath, fearing it would be a regret. His heart raced as he clicked on the message—he had been accepted! This to him was such a great opportunity. He would finally get to work on his book, *Upsurge of Cancer in Kenya: Risk factors, Pathogenesis and Feasible Preventive Measures,* during a six-month-long stay at JIAS.

As Dr. Jeff stared at the acceptance letter on his laptop screen, childhood dreams flooded back. Growing up, South Africa had always fascinated him. He had heard stories about the country, its struggles, and its heroes. More recently, he'd watched the 2010 FIFA World Cup, the first on African soil, and bought a vuvuzela to celebrate the event. He still had it tucked away, a symbol of his admiration for the country.

But one thing stood out above the rest—his deep love for South African music. Songs like Chico's *"I Need Some Money,"* Yvonne Chaka Chaka's *"Umqombothi,"* and Lucky Dube's *"Remember Me"* had been the soundtrack to his youth. As the thought of visiting Johannesburg took root, the melodies of those tracks seemed to echo in the background of his mind. His fingers instinctively tapped on the desk, and he began scribbling a list of "must-do" activities in Joburg, his excitement palpable. Quickly, he searched online, and soon enough, the soft strains of a *"Best of Lucky Dube"* mixtape filled the room in low tones, fueling his growing anticipation.

That excitement, however, was tempered when Mamatotos walked in, holding Kin's hand. She sat beside him on the couch, quick to notice the grin on his face. Always direct, she asked what was going on, and after listening to his news, her face shifted from joy to concern. "I wonder if you've really thought this through," she said softly. The weight of her words hit him. How would she manage their three children on her own? With her demanding job at the hospital, getting the kids to school, picking them up, helping with homework, and the daily grind of parenting—she was right. On top of that, she had to oversee the family farm and estate, both locally and in distant lands of Nandi. Six months was a long time.

As she spoke, Lucky Dube's *"Remember Me"* played from his phone. He listened to the lyrics for the hundredth time, and they pierced his heart. The song was about the pain of long absences from family, something he feared. But Dr. Jeff assured himself he would stay in touch—Skype calls, daily updates, and remote guidance would keep them connected. Still, had made a point he couldn't ignore.

That night, he lay in bed, thinking. He was certain the fellowship was too good to pass up, but he couldn't shake off the guilt. Then an idea hit him. What if he brought the family to Johannesburg for a vacation? He could start his fellowship and have them join him later for two weeks. The children had never flown outside Kenya, and this could be the perfect opportunity for them to experience something new. The excitement returned, and over the next few hours, he worked out the details.

The following Monday, Dr. Jeff and his family traveled to Kisumu to process their passports. Two weeks later, they made their way to Nairobi to apply for visas. They spent the night at Sagret Hotel near Integrity Centre and, by 9:00 a.m., were at the VFS Global offices, in Parkfield Building, 1st Floor, Muthangari Drive, Off Waiyaki Way, Opposite

Safaricom House, Westlands. With everything in place, Dr. Jeff knew that come April, his family would be by his side in Joburg.

Before heading to Johannesburg, he arranged a short trip with his wife, flying together from Eldoret to Nairobi to spend some quality time. Their shared moments and the warm hugs they exchanged at JKIA were deeply reassuring. The evening flight through Kigali was smooth, although there was a hiccup with immigration at the Kigali airport, where an officer unnecessarily delayed him. But soon enough, he was at OR Tambo International Airport, Johannesburg, ready for the next chapter.

At JIAS, everything was well-organized. The fellows came from various countries—Singapore, South Africa, India, the Philippines, and Kenya. JIAS is established though the collaborative efforts of the University of Johannesburg (UJ) and Nanyang Technological University in Singapore. Most fellows were novelists or storytellers, but Dr. Jeff was the only scientist, working on a non-fiction science book. The fellowship allowed for a relaxed, self-driven schedule, with meals served at set times and informal gatherings to discuss progress. Thursdays were reserved for presentations, where fellows took turns showcasing their work. Despite his busy schedule, Dr. Jeff never forgot his promise to his family. He called them daily via Skype, keeping them updated on his progress and the plans he was making for their upcoming visit.

Finally, when eight long weeks had passed, the day arrived. His family had landed in Johannesburg. Dr. Jeff arranged for an Uber driver, Akudzwe, to pick them up from OR Tambo International Airport, while he left JIAS and walked over to their cozy guest house—Resident On 3rd in Westdene—to prepare for their arrival. Collin and Shawn, the proprietors, greeted him warmly. Dr. Jeff had checked out the place a week earlier and made all the necessary payments. The house was perfect for a family retreat, with its spacious living area, two bedrooms, a well-equipped kitchen, and a beautiful outdoor pool beside a breakfast area that caught the early morning sun.

As they walked through the space, Dr. Jeff confirmed everything was in order, especially the special dinner he'd arranged for the kids, complete with a celebratory cake for their long-awaited reunion.

It wasn't long before Akudzwe's car pulled up at the guest house. Dr. Jeff' heart raced as he heard the familiar voices of his wife and children excitedly chatter outside. He rushed to the door, and there they were—Eth, Ryo, and little Kins, their faces lit up with excitement despite the long flight. The children ran into his arms, laughter filling the air as they embraced tightly.

Once inside, the family marveled at the guesthouse, especially the pool area, where they would enjoy breakfast every morning. Dinner was served shortly after, with the kids delighted by the special meal prepared just for them. Jenny, seated beside Dr. Jeff, was visibly more relaxed after their long separation, her smile wide as they caught up on everything that had happened while he was away.

They spent the evening reminiscing about the past eight weeks and discussing their plans for the days ahead. There was so much laughter, and the excitement for their Johannesburg adventure was palpable. The children eagerly shared stories from school and their excitement about exploring South Africa. Dr. Jeff filled them in on the fellowship, his work, and the fascinating people he had met at JIAS.

They all stayed up much later than they had planned, unable to contain their joy at being together again. The kids, tired from the travel but too excited to sleep, stayed up with wide eyes, making plans for the adventures that would begin the very next morning. Finally, one by one, they made their way to bed, exhausted but filled with happiness.

As Dr. Jeff and Jenny tucked the children in, they exchanged smiles. The long wait was over, and the family adventure had truly begun.

Their first adventure led them to the tranquil Johannesburg Botanical Gardens, a vast space adorned with ancient trees and scenic paths. The family strolled under the beautiful tree canopies, marveling at the number of visitors walking their pet dogs and enjoying the peaceful atmosphere. At one point, they settled on the lush lawns for a few rounds of poker with a deck of cards, the day unfolding perfectly under a soft sun peeking through the clouds.

However, as they continued their walk, a somber tone filled the air as the funeral service for Winnie Madikizela-Mandela commenced at Orlando Stadium nearby. The sounds of the loudspeakers carrying the ceremony reached the garden, subtly reminding them of the historical moment taking place. The children grew quiet, their curiosity piqued as Dr. Jeff explained the significance of the event.

He told them about Winnie's pivotal role in the liberation of South Africa, her courage, and the sacrifices she made for freedom. As the service continued, the powerful voice of Julius Malema, leader of the Economic Freedom Fighters (EFF) and a prominent figure in South Africa's political landscape, resonated through the stadium speakers. Known for his fiery speeches and deep connection to the liberation movement, Malema's address carried the weight of the nation's grief and reverence for Madikizela-Mandela. "I am here not to bury Mama because mothers don't die, they multiply into millions of red flowers of love".

The family paused their stroll, captivated by the weight of the words echoing around them. "I'm here to express my condolences to your biological children and to the rest of the Madikizela and Mandela family," Malema continued, his voice resonating with emotion. "I'm here to look at your grandchildren in the eyes and tell them that they will never be treated like they've got leprosy for as long as I'm still alive."

The powerful address continued, with Malema sharply criticizing those who had betrayed Madikizela-Mandela. "Mama, the UDF cabal is here. The cabal that rejected you, disowned you, and sent you to the brutal apartheid regime is here," he proclaimed.

As the family stood in silence, reflecting on the profound history that was being honored, the sky suddenly darkened. A heavy downpour, accompanied by fierce hailstones and loud claps of thunder, interrupted their quiet reflection.

"Run for cover!" Dr. Jeff shouted, laughter in his voice as he scooped up little Kins, who shrieked with a mix of excitement and discomfort. Eth grabbed Ryo's hand, and together they dashed toward a small shelter near the entrance, dodging puddles as the storm intensified. Soaked but exhilarated, they huddled together, the storm now blending with the sounds of the momentous farewell to South Africa's Mother of the Nation.

By the time they found refuge, they were all drenched. Kins's hair clung to her face, and Ryo wrung out the bottom of his shirt, grumbling, "Well, that was unexpected."

Dr. Jeff spotted a cozy restaurant nearby and, sensing that his family needed to warm up, ushered them inside. As they sat down at a table, the warmth of the restaurant's fireplace quickly took the chill off. They ordered steaming bowls of soup, hot chocolate for the kids, and strong coffee for Jenny and Dr. Jeff.

"Now that was an adventure," Jenny chuckled, holding her cup with both hands to soak up the warmth.

But just as the family started to relax, Jenny gasped and clutched her wrist. "My bracelet! It's gone!" she exclaimed. The bracelet, a precious family heirloom, had been a gift from her mother, and the thought of losing it was unbearable.

Without hesitation, they bundled up and headed back out into the rain, retracing their steps through the garden. After a tense search in the mud and puddles, Eth spotted a glint of gold peeking from under some wet

leaves. "Found it!" he shouted, holding up the bracelet. The family cheered, and with the rain lightening up, they headed back, wet but relieved, already laughing about their unexpected adventure.

The ride back to the guest house was filled with excitement as the kids insisted on taking a tuk-tuk, or *Shesha Tuks* as they called it locally. The small, cozy space allowed the family to squeeze together, keeping warm in the evening chill. Their driver, Lubanzi, was a lively character, cracking jokes and pointing out interesting sights along the way, much to the children's delight.

Before heading home, they made a quick stop at the Spar near JIAS to pick up groceries for the week ahead. By the time they reached the guest house, a delicious hot meal was waiting for them, just as Babakidos had arranged.

The rest of the evening was spent relaxing together, curled up in front of a giant home theatre, watching movies, and sharing laughter. It was the perfect end to their first day together in Johannesburg, and the anticipation for the adventures ahead only grew stronger.

The morning was an early rising one as they embarked on their next adventure that took them to the Johannesburg Zoo, and it was a day filled with unexpected thrills. The highlight came when they visited the primate section and encountered Mokoko, a massive, majestic gorilla.

Mokoko was sitting quietly in his enclosure, watching the visitors with calm, intelligent eyes. Kins, standing close to the glass, was completely mesmerized. "He's so big!" she whispered.

Suddenly, Mokoko moved quickly towards the glass, causing everyone to jump back in surprise. Ryo yelped, and even Dr. Jeff felt his heart skip a beat. Mokoko stood up to his full height and let out a low, rumbling grunt, then—much to everyone's relief—sat back down calmly, resuming his peaceful observation. The encounter left them all with wide eyes and fast-beating hearts, but it was a memory that would stay with them forever.

Next, they wandered into the snake park. Jenny was uneasy from the start, but the kids were eager to see the giant pythons they'd heard so much about. As they entered the dimly lit room, a massive python slid slowly across its enclosure. Ryo squealed in delight, but Kins clung to Dr. Jeff, wide-eyed.

"They won't get out, right?" Kins asked nervously, glancing up at the towering glass enclosures.

"No worries," Dr. Jeff assured him, although even he felt a twinge of discomfort at the sight of the enormous snakes coiling and uncoiling in their habitats.

They moved on quickly, finding solace in the next stop: the giant aquarium. There, the family marveled at the beautiful, graceful movements of colorful fish swimming through the water. The serene scene was a stark contrast to their previous heart-pounding moments, and they found themselves lingering, mesmerized by the underwater world.

There were countless other adventures in between, with the family dedicating plenty of time to shopping, especially at Campus Square, China Mall, and other bustling shopping centers. Time seemed to slip away faster than they could keep track of, with the first week flying by in what felt like two short days. Everyone struggled to keep count of the days as they rushed past. But even with time speeding by, Dr. Jeff had carefully lined up enough activities to make sure their stay was unforgettable.

Gold Reef City proved to be one of the biggest highlights for the family, filled with excitement and adrenaline. The real thrill, though, came with the rides. Tai, in particular, had been eyeing the towering roller coaster, the Anaconda, ever since they entered the park. Its twisted, looping track soared high above the ground, a dizzying marvel that he couldn't wait to tackle.

"You sure you're up for it?" Dr. Jeff asked with a grin, as he and were also planning to brave the ride. nodded enthusiastically, while Kins and Ryo, too small for the Anaconda, looked disappointed.

But their mood quickly lifted when they spotted a series of smaller rides just their size. While Eth joined his parents for the thrilling Anaconda, Kins and Ryo eagerly jumped on the mini roller coasters, bumper cars, and spinning teacups. Their laughter echoed through the park as they darted from ride to ride, thrilled by each new adventure.

Meanwhile, on the Anaconda, Eth felt the adrenaline rush as the roller coaster climbed higher and higher. Jenny held on tightly to Dr. Jeff's hand, laughing nervously as the ride twisted and turned at breakneck speeds. By the time they got off, their hearts were racing, but they all wore huge grins on their faces.

"That was amazing!" Eth exclaimed, his eyes sparkling with excitement.

Next, they decided to take a break from the rides and entered the 4D Theatre. Donning their special 3D glasses, they settled into their seats, eager for the immersive experience. As the film began, they were transported into a vibrant world where the action came to life around them. With every swoosh of the wind and splash of water, Kins squealed in delight, while Ryo giggled at the unexpected surprises. The whole family was swept up in the excitement, their laughter and cheers blending seamlessly with the thrilling visuals on the screen.

Emerging from the theatre, they felt exhilarated, ready to tackle more adventures in the park but once again time was not on their favour.

The day ended with ice cream and more laughter as the family recounted their favorite moments, with the Anaconda being the highlight for Eth and his parents, while Kins and Ryo couldn't stop talking about their wild bumper car ride.

Realizing that it would be impossible to cover all of Johannesburg's must-see spots in their limited time, the family decided to embark on the iconic red bus tour, a hop-on, hop-off experience that showcased the city's most famous landmarks. As the bus weaved through the bustling streets, Dr. Jeff excitedly pointed out the sprawling Johannesburg skyline, and together they admired the towering buildings that defined the city's silhouette.

One of their stops was the Carlton Centre, which, at that time, was still the tallest building in Johannesburg, standing proudly at 50 floors. Dr. Jeff explained that although it had been the tallest for decades, the Leonardo, a 55-floor skyscraper in Sandton, was nearing completion and poised to take its title. "This," Dr. Jeff remarked with a grin, "is technically the roof of Africa." As they ascended to the top of the Carlton Centre, the family was in awe of the breathtaking, bird's-eye view. From this vantage point, cars and buses below looked like miniature toys, a humbling reminder of the city's vastness.

The bus made a stop at Nelson Mandela's house in Soweto, where they got off to explore. It was a deeply moving experience for the family as they walked through the small, humble home of one of the world's greatest leaders. Eth, Ryo and Kins listened closely as their guide shared stories about Mandela's life, his imprisonment, and his fight for freedom.

From there, the family made their way to the Apartheid Museum, where the stark reality of South Africa's history was laid bare. The exhibits were powerful, and Jenny found herself holding back tears as they moved through the halls. The children, though young, could sense the gravity of the history they were witnessing.

After the museum, the family re-boarded the bus, quiet and reflective. But as they rode through the city, the somber mood slowly lifted, and by the time they reached their final stop, they were once again chatting about the rest of their plans for the trip. The day had been a mix of emotions—adventure, history, and reflection—but it was one they would never forget.

Taking the kids to the ice rink was meant to be a fun outing, but it turned into a bit of a challenge when Kins, normally full of energy, struggled to keep her balance on the ice. After several falls, she felt embarrassed and wanted to give up. But Eth and Ryo, always determined, kept going even after their own tumbles.

Seeing her elder sibling's perseverance, Kins was motivated to try again. With Dr. Jeff and Jenny cheering her on, she finally found her footing. By the end of the session, Kins was gliding across the ice confidently. The experience taught her a valuable lesson about resilience and never giving up, a memory that would stick with her long after they returned to Kenya.

When it was finally time for the family to return home, Dr. Jeff felt a pang of sadness. He escorted the family to the airport to say goodbye. He watched as the last one of them, Jenny, faded into the waiting bays. From here, he headed straight back to room number 30 at JIAS. The house was quieter, and the daily routine of his fellowship resumed. But the memories of their adventure fueled him. His writing took on new energy, and soon enough, he was making significant progress on his book.

As the months flew by, Dr. Jeff realized that not only had he grown as a writer during his fellowship, but the time spent with his family in Johannesburg had been the adventure of a lifetime. He had fallen in love with Johannesburg—the people, the place, and the experience. He knew, somehow, he would return one day.

Prof. Peter Vale, the JIAS director, had been phenomenal, as were Reshmi and Emy, the administrators, and Sieka, the chef together with all the other JIAS staff.

When his fellowship finally came to an end, he packed up his belongings, feeling a deep sense of gratitude for both the work he had accomplished and the unforgettable family journey that had made it all so special.

The End.

# The Magic Baobab Tree and the City Lights

Once upon a time, in a lively city not far from the savannah, there stood a towering baobab tree named Samuel. But Samuel was no ordinary baobab; he had a hidden gift—a quiet, magical power. His wide, sturdy branches stretched out toward the sky, and while they offered shade and shelter, they also had the ability to bring peace to anyone who sat beneath them. The people of the city admired Samuel for his size and strength, but most of all, for the calm and wisdom he exuded. His magic wasn't flashy, but those who spent time near him always left feeling lighter, their worries soothed.

Not far from Samuel's roots, the elegant city light, Troy, stood tall and proud. Troy was adored by many in the city for his brilliant radiance. He believed his brightness was the symbol of strength. "Look at me!" he would boast, flashing his dazzling rays. "I am the strongest, for no one else shines as bright as I do!"

But Samuel the baobab never envied Troy's blinding glow. He stood quietly, his leaves rustling softly in the breeze, listening to the whispers of the wind and the songs of the birds. He knew that true strength wasn't about shining the brightest; it was about standing firm, offering quiet support to those in need. His magical gift allowed him to connect with the

creatures of the forest and the wind itself, making him a keeper of wisdom beyond words.

One day, Mayor Kie decided to throw a grand banquet in honor of Samuel's humble spirit. "Samuel has given us shelter, fruit, and peace without ever boasting of his strength," Mayor Kie told the city. "It's time we celebrate his down-to-earth humility."

Troy, however, wasn't pleased. "Why would they celebrate that dull old tree when I am the one who lights up the city every night?" he grumbled, flashing his lights even brighter. Troy had heard whispers of Samuel's magic, and it only fueled his jealousy. "If I can convince the city that Samuel's magic is dangerous, I'll be the greatest," he thought.

So, Troy devised a plan. He visited Mayor Kie late at night, planting malicious ideas in the mayor's mind. "Mayor," Troy whispered, "you've heard the rumors about Samuel's magical powers, haven't you? It's said that he can control the wind and speak to the birds. Are you sure he's using this power for good? What if he's planning something else, something far more dangerous?"

Mayor Kie, though doubtful, listened carefully. "Samuel has always been a protector," he replied. "He's never shown any sign of ill will."

But Troy persisted. "What if Samuel's magic is growing stronger? What if he's plotting to take over the city? He meets with the birds at night, Mayor—who knows what they're planning? Maybe it's time to cut him down before it's too late."

The mayor hesitated, torn between his respect for Samuel and the fear Troy was stoking in his heart.

Not satisfied, Troy took his plan a step further. He spread rumors among the people, claiming that Samuel was holding secret meetings with the birds of the air, plotting to overthrow Mayor Kie. "I've seen it myself," Troy told them, "Samuel gathers with eagles, owls, and vultures. He's using his magic to control them, and soon, he'll take over the city."

The city buzzed with fear and suspicion. Some people believed Troy's lies, while others trusted Samuel's gentle nature. But the whispers grew louder, and soon the mayor's advisors began to pressure him to act. "We could sell Samuel's timber," they said, "it's valuable, and the city could make a fortune."

Samuel, unaware of the storm brewing around him, continued to stand tall and protect the city with his quiet magic. Those who sat beneath his branches still felt the peace he brought, but fewer and fewer came, wary of the rumors swirling about his powers.

The night of the banquet arrived, and as the city gathered under Samuel's shade, dark clouds rolled in, covering the sky. A fierce storm, far more powerful than any the city had ever seen, began to howl through the streets. The wind roared, tearing through the city, and rain fell in torrents. The people ran for shelter, but Troy's proud light flickered. His beams, which had once shone so brightly, dimmed in the face of the storm.

WITH A FINAL GUST OF wind, Troy's light went out, leaving the city in darkness. The people, frightened and confused, huddled under Samuel's wide branches, seeking refuge. It was then that Samuel's quiet magic truly revealed itself. His branches seemed to grow even wider, wrapping protectively around the people. His deep roots held firm against the winds, and his leaves shielded everyone from the rain.

Mayor Kie, Jonie the city clerk, Angie the Parliament speaker, and many others felt the warmth of Samuel's magic, calming their fears as they waited for the storm to pass. The birds of the air, those same creatures Troy had maligned, flew down to Samuel's branches, forming a protective shield around the tree and the people gathered beneath him.

When the storm finally subsided, the city lay in awe of the baobab's magic. Samuel had saved them all, not with flashes of brilliance, but with quiet strength, deep roots, and his connection to the natural world.

Troy, now dim and humbled, realized that his jealousy had led him astray. Mayor Kie turned to Troy, his face serious. "Troy, I need to know the truth. Did Samuel ever plan to overthrow me as you claimed?"

Troy, filled with regret, admitted everything. He confessed to spreading lies about Samuel's magic and devising the plan to cut him down for timber. "I'm sorry," Troy whispered, his once-proud beams flickering faintly. "I thought that shining the brightest was the only way to be strong. But I was wrong."

The people, hearing Troy's confession, forgave him. Mayor Kie looked at Samuel, whose magic had saved the city, and said, "Samuel's strength lies not in his magic alone, but in his humility and wisdom. Troy, you can learn from him."

Mayor Kie and the entire city were thrilled to throw a grand banquet in honor of Samuel's humble spirit. Long tables were set up beneath Samuel's sprawling branches, adorned with colorful fabrics and twinkling fairy lights. The air was filled with the delicious aroma of food and the joyous sounds of laughter and music. Samuel was beautifully decorated with garlands of flowers and twinkling lanterns hanging from his branches, creating a magical atmosphere.

As the night fell and the banquet continued, a special tribute was unveiled—a magnificent miniature statue of Samuel. The statue was crafted with great care, capturing Samuel's majestic form and wise presence. It was placed in the center of the city's square, where it still stands today. The statue has become a symbol of strength and humility, and many pilgrims come from far and wide to celebrate the incredible Samuel, honoring his legacy and the wisdom he shared with the city.

And so, the city thrived, with Samuel standing tall and Troy shining gently, a reminder to all that true strength lies in humility and the ability to weather even the fiercest of storms.

THE END.

**Book Description:**

*Stories from My Father* is a captivating collection of tales, brimming with wisdom, adventure, and life lessons. With roots in the author's own experiences, this book invites readers into diverse landscapes, from the Maasai Mara to Johannesburg, Boston, Kisumu, and beyond. Whether exploring themes of resilience, innovation, or family bonds, these stories resonate universally with readers of all ages. Each narrative not only reflects a personal journey but also speaks to the collective wisdom passed down through generations.

**About the Author:**

Dr. Geoffrey Maiyoh is an esteemed academic and a passionate storyteller. With a deep knowledge in biomedical sciences, including biochemistry and molecular biology, Dr. Maiyoh has taught and researched extensively in non-communicable diseases like cancer and diabetes. His research has been widely published in peer-reviewed journals. Dr. Maiyoh's love for storytelling transcends his scientific work, as he shares his personal experiences with readers, drawing from the rich tapestry of his life in Africa and beyond.

**Praise for Stories from My Father:**

*"A remarkable journey through storytelling, wisdom, and the beauty of family."*

*"A must-read for anyone seeking to understand the deep bonds that unite us all."*

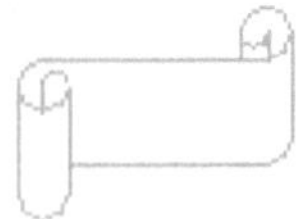

www.ingramcontent.com/pod-product-compliance
Lightning Source LLC
LaVergne TN
LVHW091224150826
845673LV00003B/1008

* 9 7 9 8 2 3 0 5 6 3 5 9 4 *